Copyright © 1990 by Tony Ross
First published by Andersen Press Ltd., London

Atheneum
Macmillan Publishing Company
866 Third Avenue, New York, NY 10022
First United States Edition 1990
Printed in Italy

10 9 8 7 6 5 4 3 2 1

Library of Congress Cataloging-in-Publication Data
Ross, Tony.
    Mrs. Goat and her seven little kids / Tony Ross.
    —1st U.S. ed.   p.   cm.
    Summary: Mother Goat rescues six of her kids after they are swallowed by a
wicked wolf.
    ISBN 0-689-31624-0
    [1. Fairy tales.   2. Folklore—Germany.]   I. Title.
PZ8.R668Mr   1990   398.24′5297358′9043—dc20
[E]   89-17933   CIP   AC

Mrs. Goat and her seven little kids

Tony Ross

ATHENEUM · 1990 · NEW YORK

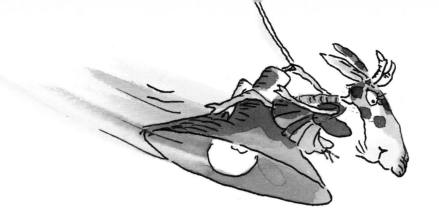

Once upon a time, Big Mother Goat was about to go to the supermarket.

"Kids," she said to her children, "don't you open that door to *anyone*. If you do, the Hungry Wolf will probably get in and eat you all. Now, we don't want that, do we?"

"No, we don't want that," said the kids.

"I'll kick him on the leg!" shouted the littlest one.

Now, the wolf was hiding underneath the window, and he heard all this. When Big Mother Goat had gone on her way, he knocked on the door.

"Who's that?" shouted the kids together.

"I'm your mom," the wolf growled. "Open up the door. I forgot to give you your pocket money."

"You're not Mom," shouted the littlest one. "Mom's got a squeaky little voice that sounds like music."

"You're the Hungry Wolf," shouted the kids, and they wouldn't open the door.

So the wolf ran off to the music teacher's house.

"Teach me to speak in a squeaky little voice like music," he growled. "If you don't, I'll bite your beak off."

"Very well," said the music teacher, and she did her best.

Then the wolf hurried back to the kids' house and banged on the door. "Let me in, this is Mommy. I've got some sweets for you," he called.

"Show us your hoof first," said the littlest one, and the wolf pushed his paw through the letterbox.

"That's not Mom's hoof," cried the kids. "Mom's hoof's white. You're the Hungry Wolf."

The littlest one hit the paw with his little hammer, and the kids refused to open the door.

"*Owwwwwwwchhhh!*" The wolf snatched his paw out of the letterbox and sucked his fingers. "White, is it?" he snarled, and went off to find an artist.

"It's got to be white, with a little black bit at the end, just like a goat's hoof," he told the artist. "Do a good job of it, and I won't bite your nose off."

The artist did a very good job, and the wolf hurried back to the house where the kids lived.

He banged on the door and shouted in a squeaky little voice like music, "Let me in, dearies. I've brought you some comics from the supermarket." The wolf waved his paw through the letterbox. "Look, it's Mommy."

"It's Mom's hoof, all right," said one of the kids.

"And it's Mom's little squeaky voice like music," said another. "Open the door."

"Not so fast . . . " said the littlest one. "Let's see your tail."

The wolf stuck his tail through the letterbox.

"Mom's tail is dainty, like a stalk of wheat," said one kid. "This tail is gray and bushy, like . . .like . . . "

"Like the Hungry Wolf's tail," cried the littlest one. "Excuse me while I bite it."

The wolf howled, and the kids refused to open the door.

"So Mom's tail is dainty, like a stalk of wheat, is it?" muttered the wolf, and he rushed off to see the dentist.

"I don't usually remove tails," said the dentist.

"If you don't remove this one, I'll bite your tail off," said the wolf.

"Then I'll make an exception in your case," said the dentist. "After all, I do have the necessary equipment. This won't hurt."

The wolf placed a stalk of wheat where his tail was and once again banged on the kids' front door.

"Let me in," he cried, in his little squeaky voice like music, waving his paw painted like a hoof. "I'm Mommy, and I've got ice cream."

He turned around and wiggled his new tail.

"It's Mom's little voice, squeaky like music," said one kid.

"It's Mom's hoof, white with a little black tip," said another.

"It's Mom's tail, dainty, like a stalk of wheat," said a third.

"It's Mom!" they all shouted joyfully, and threw open the door. All, that is, except the littlest one, who wasn't so sure, so he hopped into the coal bucket to hide.

In leaped the wolf and swallowed six little kids whole.

"I thought there were seven," grumbled the wolf. "Seven would have been delicious. Still, six is okay."

So saying, he loosened his belt and helped himself to a glass of Big Mother Goat's best root beer.

The wolf took the root beer into the back garden and sat down in a wicker chair. Then, with an awful grin on his face, he dozed in the sun.

When Big Mother Goat got home, she was laden down with seven bags of sweets, seven comics, and seven ice creams.

The littlest one jumped out of the coal bucket and told his mother exactly what had happened.

"He's still here, Mom," he bleated. "He's in the garden. He's in your chair."

"*What?*" roared Big Mother Goat, dropping all her bags. "In my chair? With my kids in him? *Let me get at him!*"

Big Mother Goat hit the dozing wolf at ninety miles an hour.

She butted him right out of the wicker chair.

She butted him so hard that one of her kids shot out of his mouth.

She butted him again and out came another.

"Not again!" pleaded the wolf, trying to crawl away. "Not on my bottom, my tail place still hurts…*ow*!"

She butted him again and out flew a third kid.

Altogether, Big Mother Goat butted the wolf seven times. Once each to get back her six swallowed children, and once to send the wolf right over the trees and away forever.

Then she gathered her kids around her, dried their tears, and gave each one a big kiss on the nose…

and a slap on the ear for opening the door to a wolf.